TAKE YOUR OCTOPUS TO SCHOOL DAY

BY Audrey Vernick

ILLUSTRATED BY Diana Schoenbrun

Alfred A. Knopf   New York

Bella

Adelaide

Ms. Crenshaw

Brody

Enzo

For my own personal superhero,
Tara Michaels (who had a pet octopus!)
—A.V.

To Daniel —D.S.

THIS IS A BORZOI BOOK PUBLISHED BY ALFRED A. KNOPF

Text copyright © 2018 by Audrey Vernick

Jacket art and interior illustrations copyright © 2018 by Diana Schoenbrun

All rights reserved. Published in the United States by Alfred A. Knopf, an imprint of

Random House Children's Books, a division of Penguin Random House LLC, New York.

Knopf, Borzoi Books, and the colophon are registered trademarks of Penguin Random House LLC.

Visit us on the Web! rhcbooks.com

Educators and librarians, for a variety of teaching tools, visit us at RHTeachersLibrarians.com

Library of Congress Cataloging-in-Publication Data is available upon request.

ISBN 978-0-399-55710-1 (trade) — ISBN 978-0-399-55711-8 (lib. bdg.) — ISBN 978-0-399-55712-5 (ebook)

The illustrations in this book were created using ink, watercolor, and charcoal pencil, with digital tweaking.

MANUFACTURED IN CHINA

September 2018   10 9 8 7 6 5 4 3 2 1   First Edition

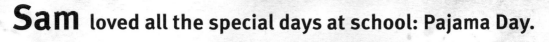

Sam loved all the special days at school: Pajama Day.

Crazy Hair Day. Dress Like Your Teacher Day.

For Silly Hat Day, he'd gone all out.

"Wish me luck," he said.

Thurgood raised a tentacle, high-fiving his best friend.

When Sam walked into his classroom, Tara whistled.

Three kids said the same thing, all in a row:

Whoa! Whoa! Whoa!

Caleb clapped.

TOOT TOOT

Then Maya walked in, wearing a hat even Dr. Seuss couldn't have dreamed up.

"Silly Hat Day is *not* a competition," Ms. Crenshaw said.

But Sam knew Maya had won.

On Super Sports-Fan Day, Sam was determined to win.
He dressed like a catcher, grabbed his baseball, and
waved good-bye to Thurgood. Thurgood waved back.

No one in class had seen a ball signed by two Sharks
outfielders before.

Then Tara walked in.

She didn't have an autographed ball, but she did have the Sharks starting shortstop, Murphy Greer, right by her side.

And so it went on Space Travel Day

and Less Famous American Presidents' Day.

Sam's costume was always really good—but someone else's was always better.

When Ms. Crenshaw announced Take Your Octopus to School Day, Sam raced home, his smile so big he caught bugs in his mouth.

He prepared the travel tank.

He prepared Thurgood, too.

"There will be lots of people. The tall ones are the teachers."

"There's nothing to be scared of, Thurgood."

"And who's going to be the best octopus ever?"

Thurgood raised a tentacle as if to say ME . . . ?

On the big day, Sam burst into the classroom. "Are you ready to see the most amazing cephalopod mollusk in the order Octopoda?!"

Everyone was gathered around Caleb's travel tank,
talking about something called Hank.

"Wait a minute . . . ," Sam said. "That's not an octopus. That's a squid!"

"THIS," he said, wheeling in the travel tank, "is Thurgood, my octopus."

Everyone looked.

Sam waited for the oohs and aahs,
the whoas and whistles.

But it was silent. Until Bella asked,
"Where?"

Thurgood was gone!

Sam raced back outside. Did Thurgood slide out when they rolled up the ramp? Nope.

Back in the classroom, Sam was in a panic!

"Has anyone seen Thurgood?"

"What does he look like?" Menachem asked.

"An octopus!" Sam yelled.

Sam's heart beat faster, faster, faster.

"Don't worry," Caleb said. "Just stand right by the tank. Let him see you."

"No, I have to—" But in that very instant, Thurgood . . .

incredibly . . .

wondrously . . .

appeared.

Everyone gathered
around Thurgood's tank,
oohing, aahing.

Whistling. Whoaing.

"WHAT?" Sam said. "What was THAT?"

"Camouflage!" Caleb said. "Hank's good at it, too."

"Thurgood's never done that before!"

"Maybe he's never been scared before."

Sam felt an idea bubbling to the surface . . .

Caleb said he'd help. Thurgood and Hank could help, too.

And on Camouflage Day, the four of them did a multi-part, multi-media, multi-pet presentation.

Everyone said it was multi-incredible!

But no one knew for sure who won Camouflage Day.

Because no one could see them.